D1605332

Kids Training Puppies
in 5 Minutes

by
JoAnn Dahan

Puppy Paw Press
Asbury

Puppy Paw Press
Asbury, NJ 08802
www.kidstrainingpuppies.com

Printed in China by Everbest Through Four Colour Imports, Ltd., Louisville, KY

1 3 5 7 9 10 8 6 4 2

JoAnn's Dedication

For my husband whose constant love and support has made this book possible.

To my children, Paul and Emily, who have helped me train dogs and puppies since they were babies.

A special squeeze and kiss on the muzzle for Tilly, she's the best.

Walter's Dedication

I was very honored and excited when JoAnn asked me to create the images for her book. Thank you JoAnn for allowing me this great experience.

Most of all I would like to thank my wife Gloria, for putting up with the endless last minute "just one more shot!," and the editing of countless images. Her creative support is the backbone of the images within this book.

I would also like to thank my children, Dillon, Denver, Jenna and Christine for giving me the inspiration and energy to see things through a child's eye.

Acknowledgements

A special thanks to Walter for his brilliant photography and hard work and to his wife Gloria for putting up with my endless phone calls.

To my wonderful Veterinarian, Dr. Vincent Zaccheo and staff at Warren Animal Hospital for allowing us to film such great photos for our book.

Thanks to all our little trainers who will some day grow up to be great trainers:
Emily and Paul Dahan, Virginia Kutsop, Jenna and Christine George, Katlynne, Victoria and Ryan Dahan.

Andrea Robertson for the use of her handsome yellow puppy, Accolades Continuous Odyssey Otis.
Thanks to Chris, Christopher, Austin and Morgan Hamler.
Daria Butka for the use of her beautiful litter.

To my good friends at The Greater Lehigh Valley Writers Group who when asked, were there to help.

Trish Becker who added just the right touches to the book.

Adrienne Kaczynski whose cover design made this dream real.

To become great dogs puppies need to be trained.
I know that children can care for and train their puppy.

This book was written just for them.

Tips to Follow

- While training with this book, you will use your puppy's name, instead of *Sam*.

- Remember puppies are little so when you're training, be sure to hold the treat at their level, otherwise you'll find the puppy will jump up.

- Use treats that are easy to swallow such as: small pieces of cheese or 1/4" hot dog slices.

- Do not to overtrain your puppy, always leave your puppy wanting more. Five-minute sessions are long enough.

- Your puppy will learn fast so don't rush him/her.

- Only train one command a week.

- Always remember to praise your puppy when he has done a command correctly by saying, "Good puppy!"

- Don't forget to release your puppy or free your puppy by saying, "Free! or OK!"

- Repeat a command if the puppy did not do the command correctly.

- When you complete a training session, play with your puppy. Make training a positive experience.

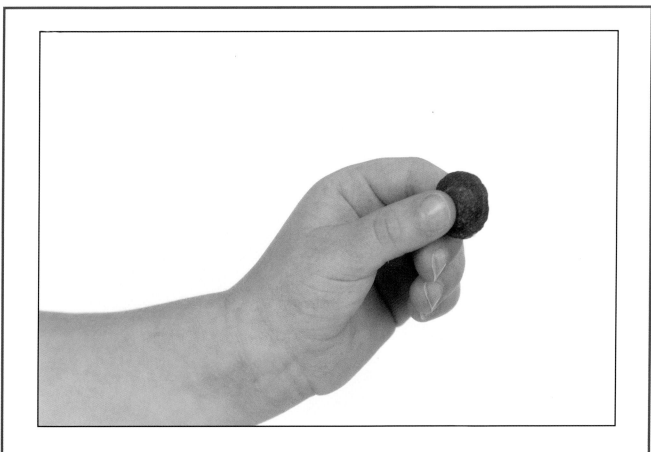

When you are training with your puppy hold the treat loosely between your thumb and index finger.

Remember:
Be sure to hold the treat down low at the puppy's level. If you hold the treat too high the puppy will jump up to get the treat.

Train 5 minutes a day, I know you will do great.

Remember to use soft easy-to-swallow treats.

Little pieces of cheese or...

1/4" hot dog slices. You can also cook them on a paper towel on high in the microwave for 3 minutes for easy storage.

Little pieces of soft
doggie treats.

Pieces of kibble or
doggie food can also
be used.

When puppies are born their eyes and ears are sealed shut.

The mother stays near her puppies.

A puppy's eyes and ears will open at about 13 days.

Puppies go to their new homes when they are 8 weeks old.

Puppy training starts right
away.

House Breaking

When you wake up, take your puppy outside. Once outside say,
"Hurry, Sam, hurry."
This will help your puppy go potty. When your puppy goes potty say,
"Good Sam."

(Remember to use your puppy's name.)

A puppy will have to go potty shortly after you feed him.

Sam Sit!

Stand in front of Sam
with a treat.

Place the treat near
Sam's nose.

Move the treat toward
Sam's back and say,
"Sam sit!"

(You will use your dog's name.)

When Sam sits say,
"Good sit Sam."
Give Sam the treat.

(Only give Sam a treat if he does
what you ask.)

After you train 'The Sit', praise your puppy and say, "Good sit Sam. Free!"

Always let Sam know he is done training by saying, "Free, or Ok."

(Start over if he doesn't do what you ask.)

Sam Down!

Place a treat near Sam's nose.

Slowly move the treat to the ground/floor...

then slowly to you and
say, "Sam, down."

(Do not let the puppy have the
treat until he lies down. This may
take a few minutes so be patient.
If he should take the food
before lying down, start again.)

When Sam lies down say,
"Good down Sam!" Give Sam
the treat and be happy.

(Only give Sam a treat if he lies
down.)

After you train 'The Down'
say, "Good down Sam, Free!"

(Start over if he doesn't do what
you ask.)

Sam Come!

Place a treat near Sam's nose.

Back away from Sam

and say,

"Sam come!"

When Sam comes to you say,
"Good come Sam!"
Give Sam the treat.

(Only give Sam a treat if he comes to you.)

After you train 'The Come'
say,
"Good come Sam. Free!"

(Start over if he doesn't do what you ask.)

Sam Stay!

With Sam on your left, place your right hand open in front of Sam's face and say, "Sam stay!"

Step in front of Sam and say, "Sam stay!"

Count 1, 2, 3, 4, 5, 6, 7, 8, 9, 10.
If Sam did not move say,
"Good stay Sam!"
Give Sam a treat and be
happy.

After you train 'The Stay'
say, "Good stay Sam. Free!"

(Start over if he doesn't do what
you ask.)

Sam Heel!

With *Sam* on your left side, hold the treat in your right hand, then place the treat near his nose.

Step off with your left leg keeping the treat in front of the puppy say, "Sam heel!"

Keep moving say,
"Heel!"

Slow down to a stop.

Give Sam the treat and say,
"Good heel Sam!"

After you train
'The Heel' say,
"Good heel Sam. Free!"
Then play with
your puppy.

Keep Your Puppy Busy!

When puppies are bored they will chew on things you might not want them to.

Give your puppy his toy to chew on.

Socialize Your Puppy.

Include your puppy in daily
activities.

When you can, take your
puppy with you.

Bring your puppy to
after school activities.

Feed your puppy
and he will
love you more.

Puppies are

so happy

when they are with you...

JoAnn and Tilly

About the Author

JoAnn Dahan has owned many pure bred dogs and mixed breeds. She has raised, trained and bred Labrador Retrievers for 15 years. Her labs have hunting titles and have been seen in advertisements, on greeting cards, in two major motion pictures and on HBO's "The Sopranos." She and her family and four legged friends reside in Asbury, New Jersey.

About the Photographer

Walter George has a Bachelor of Fine Arts degree from the University of the Arts, Philadelphia. He specializes in children and family portraiture. His studio is located in Martinsville, New Jersey.

Walter and Sam